AF594408

SNEAK PEEK
@ SNEAKERS
REEBOK
Reebok
Kerrily Sapet

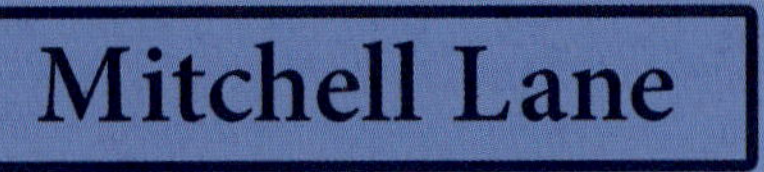

PUBLISHERS

mitchelllane.com

2001 SW 31st Avenue
Hallandale, FL 33009

First Edition, 2021.
Author: Kerrily Sapet
Designer: Ed Morgan
Editor: Sharon F. Doorasamy

Series: Sneak Peek @ Sneakers
Title: Reebok / by Kerrily Sapet

Hallandale, FL : Mitchell Lane Publishers, [2021]

Library bound ISBN: 978-1-68020-653-1
eBook ISBN: 978-1-68020-654-8

PHOTO CREDITS: cover: Shutterstock, p. 5 DYLAN MARTINEZ/REUTERS/Newscom, p. 6 KIERAN DOHERTY/REUTERS/Newscom, p. 8 Shutterstock, p. 11 Shutterstock, p. 13 Alandmanson CC-BY-SA-4.0, p. 15 Shutterstock, p. 16 Lee Young Ho/Sipa USA/Newscom, p. 19 ReebokUSA CC-BY-SA-4.0, pp. 20-21 Reebok/Cover Images/Newscom, p. 22 Shutterstock, p. 23 NASA, p. 25 Alamy, pp. 26-27 Alamy, p. 28 Shutterstock, p 29 20TH CENTURY FOX / Album/Newscom

CONTENTS

chapter 1

SENSATIONAL SHOES

The neighborhood tennis courts were cracked and crumbling. That didn't bother Venus Williams. She learned to play tennis anyway. She practiced her swing using a shopping cart filled with tennis balls. Venus was a tennis star by the time she was eight years old. People wanted her autograph before she could even write cursive. Venus got faster and stronger as she grew older. People nicknamed her "Queen V."

In 2000, Venus advanced to the finals at Wimbledon. Wimbledon is one of the biggest tournaments in tennis. Venus rocketed balls across the net. She smashed them into the corners of the court. Venus won! A few months later, she earned two gold medals at the Olympics. During Venus's career, she won at Wimbledon ten times. She also won four Olympic gold medals. "My life is one dream coming true after another," Venus said.

Venus Williams celebrates after defeating Swiss player Martina Hingis during their quarterfinal match at the Wimbledon Tennis Championships in 2000.

chapter 1

Venus played on grass, clay, and rubber tennis courts. She needed shoes that wouldn't slip and that kept her feet cool. Reebok made custom shoes for Venus. The lightweight shoes had rubber soles that gripped the court. Rubber hexagons on the soles provided cushioning. They bounced back into shape as Venus ran. Most tennis shoes were white. Venus's shoes had hot pink zigzags. The shoes became so popular that Reebok named them the Venus Trainer.

Venus Williams parades around center court at Wimbledon after winning the women's final in 2000.

Some of the first athletic shoes were made for tennis. In 1517, King Henry VIII of England played tennis wearing special leather shoes. Long ago, shoes protected people's feet from snow and hot sand. Shoes were made from animal skins, wood, and metal. People added grass for cushioning and warmth.

In 1745, a French scientist visited Peru. He discovered a white tree sap. Native people used it to make bouncy balls and sandals. He brought samples back to France. People named it rubber. They started making shoes from rubber and a thick material called canvas. But rubber soles got sticky and soft in the summer. They hardened and cracked in the winter. In 1839, Charles Goodyear combined melted rubber with chemicals to make stronger, flexible rubber. He named it **vulcanized rubber**. Vulcan was the Roman god of fire.

More people started wearing rubber and canvas shoes. They called them "sneakers." The soles were so quiet that people could sneak around. Today, sneakers are the most popular shoes in the world. Everyone from athletes to grandparents wears them. In 2017, people in the United States spent $19.6 billion on sneakers. Many of those sneakers were made by Reebok.

FAST FACT:

Archaeologists discovered a 9,000-year-old shoe at a cave in Oregon. The shoe was made from tree bark and plants woven together.

TENNIES, TRAINERS, AND TAKKIES

People around the world call sneakers by different names. In the eastern United States, they're "sneakers." In the Midwest, they're "tennis shoes." Sneakers are also known as "gym shoes," "kicks," "daps," "gutties," and "plimsolls" because early rubber-soled shoes had a stripe like a line called a "plimsoll" on a boat. Whatever the name, they're the most popular shoes on Earth.

chapter 2

OVER THE CANDY SHOP

The Reebok company started with Joseph William Foster. Foster was born in 1881 in Bolton, England. When he was old enough, he trained to become a cobbler. Foster loved to run. He started designing running shoes when he was 14 years old. Foster worked in his bedroom above his father's candy shop. He made lightweight leather shoes and drove nails down through the soles. The spiky nails would grip the ground. Athletes could push off with their toes and run faster. Foster made some of the first spiked running shoes in history. People called them "running pumps." Runners and soccer players loved them.

In 1900, Foster opened a small shoe factory called Olympic Works. Four years later, a runner wearing Foster's shoes set a world record. Athletes around the world wanted shoes designed by Foster. They sent Foster measurements of their feet, and he made custom shoes. Foster's sons, John and James, began working at the company. They renamed the company J. W. Foster and Sons.

During World War II, J. W. Foster and Sons made boots for the British army. After the war, John continued to make hand-sewn shoes. James started making machine-sewn shoes. They argued about which was better. Joseph Foster's grandsons, Jeff and Joe, joined the business after the war. After a few years, Jeff and Joe wanted to try new ideas. In 1958, they started their own shoe company. They called the company Reebok.

chapter 2

At first, Reebok made shoes for cyclists. They didn't want to compete with J. W. Foster and Sons. Jeff and Joe rented a leaky old building. At first, the brothers did the sewing themselves. They bought used shoemaking machines. The heavy machines made the old floor sag. They found bright red, yellow, and orange leather on sale. People liked their new designs. "You're a wizard," one runner told Jeff.

The Foster family has been making shoes for more than 100 years. It began with Joseph Foster making shoes in a room over his father's candy shop. Today, Reebok is one of the biggest sneaker companies in the world.

CHOOSING A NAME

A "reebok" is a speedy African antelope with sharp horns. Jeff and Joe needed a name for their new company. They found the word "reebok" in a dictionary that Joe won as a prize. Sneaker companies often pick animal names and zippy words for designs. Words such as "puma," "lightning," "zoom," and "fury" sound speedy, strong, and fast.

chapter 3

A NEW CRAZE

At first, people wore sneakers when they played sports. Then they realized sneakers were comfortable and less expensive than leather shoes. People started wearing sneakers for sports and fashion. In the 1980s, aerobics became popular. Women especially liked the fast workouts with dance moves and music. Reebok designed a lightweight, soft leather sneaker for aerobics. They called it the "Freestyle." The sneaker was a hit. Women didn't just wear them for aerobics. They wore them everywhere. In four years, Reebok's sales increased from $3 million to $900 million.

Today, sneakers come in all sizes, shapes, and colors. They fit tiny feet, big feet, and all sizes in between. There are low-cut, high-top, knee-high, and even high-heeled sneakers. They lace, Velcro, slip on, zip, and snap. Sneakers are made in a rainbow of colors. They come in everything from white to purple with zebra stripes.

Reebok competes with companies, such as Nike, to release new designs and styles. Companies make sneakers for nearly every sport, from running to gymnastics. Reebok, like many companies, also sells sportswear with its **logo** on it. In 2005, Adidas purchased Reebok. They continue to make Reebok sneakers.

chapter 3

Sneaker companies **sponsor** athletes to help sell their sneakers. They pay athletes to wear and advertise their sneakers. Reebok has worked with athletes such as Venus Williams, Shaquille O'Neal, and Peyton Manning. Companies partner with musicians and celebrities to design sneakers in the latest fashions.

Most sneaker companies, such as Reebok, make their sneakers in China and Korea. From the factory, sneakers are loaded onto trains, planes, and ships. They are sent to nearly every country in the world. People walk through jungles, run on beaches, and exercise in space wearing sneakers. Speedy robotic shoe factories can produce 1 million shoes a year.

Shaquille O'Neal attends a Reebok promotional event in Seoul, South Korea.

Sneakers are a big business. In 2018, Reebok sold $1.7 billion of sneakers. Experts predict that by 2025, people worldwide will spend $95 billion on sneakers a year. That's a lot of sneakers!

FAST FACT:

At first, Reebok's logo was the Union Jack, the United Kingdom's flag. Today, Reebok's logo looks like a black "X."

chapter 4

SNEAKER TECH

Designing and making a new sneaker takes months. It starts with a **designer** thinking about the person wearing the shoe. Basketball players need sneakers with ankle support. The soles need to grip the wooden court. Soccer players need shoes that won't slip on wet grass.

A team of designers, artists, and testers work together. They think about comfort, fit, weight, style, and materials. Sneakers are made from fabric, leather, plastic, rubber, and **synthetics**. Synthetics are combinations of man-made materials. Designers use gels, foams, beads, and air bubbles to add cushioning. In 1989, Reebok created an **innovative** sneaker called the "Reebok Pump." People could push a spot that inflated air bags inside the sneaker. "It would sort of lock your foot into the shoe," said reporter Chris Danforth. Artists add colors, patterns, and eye-catching designs to sneakers.

chapter 4

Sneaker designers are often inspired by nature. A Japanese designer studied the suckers on an octopus's tentacles. He created sneaker soles with suction cup shapes that gripped the ground. Another designer studied insect wings and leaves. He used similar patterns and shapes to develop strong, lightweight shoes. Designers are even using fake spider-web silk to make fabric for sneakers.

Reebok plans to launch its first-ever plant-based performance running shoe in 2020. The Forever Floatride GROW is part of the brand's commitment to reduce the use of petroleum-based plastics in footwear.

Designers are creating shoes that are better for the environment. Reebok's Cotton + Corn shoes use cotton fabric and rubber made from corn. Reebok also makes sneakers with fabric from Thread International. Thread International collects plastic water bottles. They shred them into flakes that can be used to make fabric. Other companies make recyclable shoes from plastic scooped from the ocean. Companies are using old tires, fishing nets, and kelp to make sneakers.

chapter 4

Designers are testing new ways of making sneakers. They use 3D printing to print **prototypes** and custom designs. Engineers at Reebok program robots to create shoes. The robots use a goopy liquid rubber and draw in 3D layers. "Liquid Factory is not just a new way of making things," said Dan McInnis. McInnis is a former NASA engineer. "It's a new speed of making things."

Today's shoes can connect to phone apps. They can measure an athlete's performance, display pictures, and lace themselves. They can even open vents to cool down sweaty feet. Sneakers are more than just fabric and rubber on your feet!

FROM SPACESUITS TO SNEAKERS

Technology developed by NASA, the National Aeronautics and Space Administration, has changed life on Earth. NASA scientists developed a process called "blow rubber molding" to create lightweight, strong space helmets. Today, shoe companies use blow rubber molding to make sneakers with soles that can be filled with shock-absorbing materials. Millions of sneaker wearers walk in astronaut-inspired shoes every day.

chapter 5

STYLISH KICKS

Look down at someone's feet and chances are that they're wearing sneakers. Everyone from toddlers to grandmas in grocery stores wears sneakers. Kids wear them in gym class. Famous actors accept awards while wearing fancy sneakers.

Sometimes people choose the same sneakers their favorite athlete or celebrity wears. In the 1980s, kids wanted the sneakers basketball star Michael Jordan wore. Wearing Air Jordans showed they could be famous one day too. "Sneakers can represent something," said Daryl McDaniels of the hip-hop band Run-DMC. "It's about people who represent a culture that doesn't only look good but people who go out of their way to do good."

Michael Jordan's shoes have a very special place in pop culture. For people who collect sneakers, Jordans are among the most prized footwear they can own.

chapter 5

Sneaker companies have **slogans** such as "Just Do It" and "I Am What I Am." The slogans inspire athletes to run farther and faster. They also encourage people to be proud of themselves. Sneakers appear in commercials, in TV shows, and in movies. Bands drop the names of sneakers in their songs. Stars post pictures on social media of themselves wearing certain sneakers.

Sneaker companies work with athletes, musicians, and celebrities to create designs. Reebok partners with Jay-Z, Victoria Beckham, Cardi B, and Ariana Grande. They also make themed shoes, such as Toy Story and Avengers sneakers.

New sneaker releases sometimes sell out fast. Fans often wait in lines for hours at stores. Websites crash as people rush to buy the new design. Reebok sold 10,000 pairs of Jay-Z's first sneaker in a few hours.

PERSON'S
GHT CAN
TRIFY
Reebok
EBOK
ARIANA GRANDE | ARTIST, SOCIAL
REEBOK.COM/BE

Sneakers are so popular that some people have closets full of them. Shoe collectors, nicknamed "sneakerheads," trade, buy, and sell shoes. They sometimes spend thousands of dollars on a pair of sneakers.

People started designing sneakers for sports more than 100 years ago. They wanted shoes that gripped hard tracks, grassy fields, and muddy trails. Today's sneakers use technology inspired by animals and spacesuits. They combine sports and fashion. There are approximately 8 billion people in the world. Many of them work and play in sneakers. A lot of those sneakers are made by Reebok.

ALIEN STOMPERS

People often notice the sneakers actors wear. In 1986, Reebok designed the "Alien Stomper" for the movie *Aliens*. The puffy grey and red high tops had thick Velcro straps. In 2017, Reebok designed a new version that glowed in the dark. It had shiny black leather to look like a slimy alien. The sneakers sold out, just like in 1986.

GLOSSARY

designer
A person who creates original products

innovative
New and different

logo
A picture or symbol

prototype
The first design or model

slogan
A saying used to advertise an item

sponsor
A company that pays someone to advertise or wear their product

synthetics
Man-made materials

vulcanized rubber
Rubber mixed with chemicals to become stronger

TIMELINE

1881 Joseph William Foster is born.

1900 Joseph William Foster founds Olympic Works; he later changes the name to J. W. Foster and Sons.

1958 Jeff and Joe Foster start Reebok.

1982 Reebok releases the "Freestyle" sneaker.

1986 Reebok's sales reach $900 million.

1989 Reebok releases the "Reebok Pump."

2003 Reebok partners with Jay-Z.

2005 Adidas buys Reebok.

2017 Reebok partners with Ariana Grande.

FURTHER READING

Buckley, James. *Who Are Venus and Serena Williams?* New York, NY: Penguin Publishing, 2017.

Cole, Jason. *Golden Kicks: The Shoes that Changed Sport*. New York, NY: Bloomsbury Sport, 2016.

Keyser, Amber J. *Sneaker Century: A History of Athletic Shoes*. Minneapolis, MN: Twenty-First Century Books, 2015.

Le Maux, Mathieu. *1000 Sneakers: A Guide to the World's Greatest Kicks, from Sport to Street*. New York, NY: Rizzoli Publications, 2016.

Nelson, Robin. *From Leather to Basketball Shoes*. Minneapolis, MN: Lerner Publishing Group, 2014.

ABOUT THE AUTHOR

Kerrily Sapet has written more than 30 books for children. Sapet wears sneakers whether she's at home, at work, or outdoors. She once owned a pair of white Reebok Freestyle sneakers.